Christmas Music

Ten Poems of Comfort and Joy

Candlestick Press

Published by:
Candlestick Press,
Diversity House, 72 Nottingham Road, Arnold, Nottingham NG5 6LF
www.candlestickpress.co.uk

Design and typesetting by Craig Twigg

Printed by Bayliss Printing Company Ltd of Worksop, UK

Donation to Our Dementia Choir
www.ourdementiachoir.com

ISBN 978 1 913627 44 7

Acknowledgements

The poems in this pamphlet are reprinted from the following books, all by permission of the publishers listed unless stated otherwise. Every effort has been made to trace the copyright holders of the poems published in this book. The editor and publisher apologise if any material has been included without permission, or without the appropriate acknowledgement, and would be glad to be told of anyone who has not been consulted.

Thanks are due to all the copyright holders cited below for their kind permission.

Maggie Anderson, *Cold Comfort* (University of Pittsburgh Press, 1986). Hayden Carruth, *Collected Shorter Poems 1946-1991* (Copper Canyon Press, 1992). Copyright © 1985 by Hayden Carruth. Reprinted with the permission of The Permissions Company, LLC on behalf of Copper Canyon Press, www.coppercanyonpress.org. Lorraine Mariner, poem first appeared in this pamphlet. Adrian Mitchell, *Come on Everybody: Poems 1953-2008* (Bloodaxe Books, 2012) www.bloodaxebooks.com. Edwin Morgan, *Collected Poems* (Carcanet Press, 1996).

All permissions cleared courtesy of Dr Suzanne Fairless-Aitken –
Swift Permissions swiftpermissions@gmail.com.

Where poets are no longer living, their dates are given.

Contents **Page**

Introduction	*Lorraine Mariner*	*5*
Winter Listening	*Adrian Mitchell*	*7*
I Heard a Bird Sing	*Oliver Herford*	*8*
From In Singing Weather	*Maggie Anderson*	*9*
Song: The Young Man with the Guitar, Testing	*Hayden Carruth*	*10*
The Singing Stars	*Marjorie Wilson*	*11*
Christmas Eve	*Christina Rossetti*	*12*
Trio	*Edwin Morgan*	*13*
The Disappointed Carol Singers	*Frances Ridley Havergal*	*14*
Sunshine and Shadow	*Paul Laurence Dunbar*	*15*
Fairytale of New York – The Pogues, featuring Kirsty MacColl	*Lorraine Mariner*	*16*

Introduction

Christmas seems to arrive earlier each year but it's not until the radio starts playing Christmas hits that I allow myself to give in at the supermarket and buy a box of mince pies. When the radio stops playing Christmas music I do feel a bit bereft.

For me, music is an essential part of Christmas. Rehearsing Christmas carols from September through to December may get a bit wearing for choirs of all ages (Victorian poet and hymnwriter Frances Ridley Havergal's 'Disappointed Carol Singers' have been practising "For many a week before") but hearing a carol years later can take us back to those feelings of wonder and anticipation we had singing in our school nativity play.

In winter nature has quietened down so we need to make our own music. Adrian Mitchell listens carefully and hears magical sounds, while the snow-hushed hills in Maggie Anderson's poem create a "singing weather" that brings the voices of those she has lost back to her on the winter wind. I've written about a Christmas song that reminds me of my father and makes me feel close to him when I hear it each year.

In Edwin Morgan's poem the "Monsters of the year" are fended off when he encounters a festive young trio on the street. Whichever Christmas music you prefer, choirs or popstars, classical or cheesy, I hope these poems will remind you of the joy and comfort that music can bring us at Christmas.

Lorraine Mariner

Winter Listening

Humble, crumbly song of the snails.
Pinecones rattling in a stormy tree.
The frosty voices of December stars.
Dragon-roaring of a factory.

Honking slapstick of seals at play.
The creak and slish of snow off a roof.
Crackle-whisper of Christmas paper.
The silver step of a unicorn's hoof.

Adrian Mitchell (1932 – 2008)

I Heard a Bird Sing

I heard a bird sing
In the dark of December.
A magical thing
And sweet to remember.

"We are nearer to Spring
Than we were in September,"
I heard a bird sing
In the dark of December.

Oliver Herford (1860 – 1935)

From In Singing Weather

7

Even the breathless dead seem,
sometimes, nevertheless, to sing.

At last it's snowed and hushed the hills,
all the forest veins revealed.

The December sky is generous once more
with a light tender as a ragtime piano

frowsy as the woman who plays it by ear
and tilts her head. She's hard as nails.

Her hands build bookcases and every ivory shelf thrums,
as she jumps all her tricky sweetness off the stool

and onto the floor. She sings in a frolic fast
as a running heart, each note wound to every other.

After long silence, there is music again,
thin lip of moon and again bright stars,

the weeds, safe now in their coffins of ice,
in singing weather. The pets of my childhood

nose the white drifts in bright collars
and bows and I whistle them home to me,

in from the cold. Now the formal dead
can love me back, with their voices

carried on the wind. And I can hold them,
rock them in my own melodic arms.

Maggie Anderson

Song: The Young Man with the Guitar, Testing

The young man with the guitar, testing new riffs
with harmonic variations, sat in the maroon
wingback chair in front of the Christmas tree,
a very good tree this year, shapely and full,
and beyond the window, its glass set in a zinc
lattice, I saw a mockingbird perched in the snow
that clung to the yew tree. The bluesy tune,
the bird, and the two trees were like ifs and buts
in a fiercely complicated discourse in my head.
The young man was Dave, my son, whom I call the Bo.

And I said nothing. What words were there to say?
Mutability, you are the existing of all things
in this actual world, and without you every day
would be today, fixed and intolerable—so
my friends tell me over and over. They take
grace and joy from the existing that I do not
easily find or respond to, for a great sorrow
holds my mind. Then let me change!—for the sake
of the trees, symbolic and natural, the bird that sings,
and a young man, Dave, my son, whom I call the Bo.

That was the year's last afternoon. Now midnight
strikes. The young man, who likes to be called Dave,
has gone out with his friends. The firelight
flickers and dwindles, the bird sleeps in the snow.
Should I also call him Dave? The new year
has come, I'm foolish and old, I think I am
vanishing, and he is the wise one now and true
in himself—as I was once long years ago.
Turn off the tree. But how strong is this dark love,
young man, my Dave, my son, whom I call the Bo!

Hayden Carruth (1921 – 2008)

The Singing Stars

All the stars tonight are singing,
As this midnight now draws near.
So the bells of heaven were ringing
On that midnight, sweet and clear.

And we hear again the story,
That with telling ne'er grows dim,
Feel our hearts stirred by its sweetness,
Kneel in worship now to Him.

Through the ages, the refrain comes,
Wondrous now, as it was then,
And the silver stars keep singing,
"Peace on earth! Good will toward men!"

Marjorie Wilson (1885 – 1934)

Christmas Eve

Christmas hath a darkness
  Brighter than the blazing noon,
Christmas hath a chillness
  Warmer than the heat of June,
Christmas hath a beauty
  Lovelier than the world can show:
For Christmas bringeth Jesus,
  Brought for us so low.

Earth, strike up your music,
  Birds that sing and bells that ring;
Heaven hath answering music
  For all Angels soon to sing:
Earth, put on your whitest
  Bridal robe of spotless snow:
For Christmas bringeth Jesus,
  Brought for us so low.

Christina Rossetti (1830 – 1894)

Trio

Coming up Buchanan Street, quickly, on a sharp winter evening
a young man and two girls, under the Christmas lights –
The young man carries a new guitar in his arms,
the girl on the inside carries a very young baby,
and the girl on the outside carries a chihuahua.
And the three of them are laughing, their breath rises
in a cloud of happiness, and as they pass
the boy says, 'Wait till he sees this but!'
The chihuahua has a tiny Royal Stewart tartan coat like a teapot-holder,
the baby in its white shawl is all bright eyes and mouth like favours
in a fresh sweet cake,
the guitar swells out under its milky plastic cover, tied at the neck
with silver tinsel tape and a brisk sprig of mistletoe.
Orphean sprig! Melting baby! Warm chihuahua!
The vale of tears is powerless before you.
Whether Christ is born, or is not born, you
put paid to fate, it abdicates
under the Christmas lights.
Monsters of the year
go blank, are scattered back,
can't bear this march of three.
– And the three have passed, vanished in the crowd
(yet not vanished, for in their arms they wind
the life of men and beasts, and music,
laughter ringing them round like a guard)
at the end of this winter's day.

Edwin Morgan (1920 – 2010)

The Disappointed Carol Singers

Oh, must we not sing our Christmas hymn,
And will you not hear our song?
With joyous voice, but with weary limb,
We have roamed the whole day long!

We have thought of the merry Christmas time
For many a week before,
And have gleefully learnt our Christmas rhyme
To carol at your door.

There are no merry larks to wake you now,
No blackbirds in woody dell;
The nightingale loves not the leafless bough,
The humming bee sleeps in his cell.

Oh, winter is gloomy and dark enough,
And must it be silent too?
Are the chorus of winds and the storm-song rough
The only sweet music for you?

But we are the birds of the winter day,
When all else is dark and still;
Then, lady, send us not all away,
And with sorrow our eager hearts fill.

Oh, do not thus wave your beautiful hand,
And bid us unheard to go;
For the carolling time of our little band
Comes but once a year, you know.

Frances Ridley Havergal (1836 – 1879)

Sunshine and Shadow

Oh, who would be sad tho' the sky be a-graying,
And meadow and woodlands are empty and bare;
For softly and merrily now there come playing,
The little white birds thro' the winter-kissed air.

The squirrel's enjoying the rest of the thrifty,
He munches his store in the old hollow tree;
Tho' cold is the blast and the snow-flakes are drifty
He fears the white flock not a whit more than we.

Chorus:

Then heigho for the flying snow!
Over the whitened roads we go,
With pulses that tingle,
And sleigh-bells a-jingle
For winter's white birds here's a cheery heigho!

Paul Laurence Dunbar (1872 – 1906)

Fairytale of New York – The Pogues, featuring Kirsty MacColl

The only Christmas song I can listen to
any day of the year, and when I do,
I think about my father and the tin whistle
he bought me one half-birthday
from the music shop near his office.

During the worst of The Troubles
my grandma tried not to speak out loud
in London so strangers wouldn't hear
her accent. But this song, when the accordion,
banjo, drum and cittern kick in,

marked a turning point for my family,
led to the leprechaun magnet with the words
It's great to be Irish! across his green belly,
picked up by my dad at Dublin airport
to live on the fridge during my teenage years.

I could have been someone. Well so
could anyone. It got him, gets me, every time.
Will they stay together? The outro plays,
it's Christmas Eve, and though I never did
I'm waltzing in my father's arms.

Lorraine Mariner

TO
JESSICA,
LOVE FROM
....

Hi, I'm JESSICA! What's your name?

On a normal street like yours and mine,
It was a bright and sunny day.
Jessica saw, as she opened the door,
A gang of animals waiting to play.

The tiger loves taking centre stage,
He's quite the confident one.
But equally, and I'm sure you'll agree,
His shy friends are also fun.

Let'sss play,
JESSICA!

Hide-and-seek's a favourite game,
It's Jessica versus giraffes.
Her careful disguise won't fool their eyes,
And it ends with smiles and laughs.

Here we come,
JESSICA!

Some friends like to relax and snuggle,
Others creep about and are tickly.
The otters hug, the gorillas are snug,
And the porcupines are cute and prickly.

Wanna hug, JESSICA?

The sloths love hanging out and snoozing,
While the monkeys swing about.
Jessica grins at the jumps and spins,
And the wild and cheeky shouts.

ZZzzzz

It's time to settle down for lunch,
Jessica's takes some beating.
Her friends have FRUITS,

GRASS, GRUBS and ROOTS,

There's an icky stench wafting
through the air,
And Jessica's turning greener!
It might just be, the hippo, you see,

Or perhaps the RING-TAILED LEMUR?!

Jessica spots the rhinos squabbling,
They're bickering and butting their heads.
She must put a stop, to their childish strop,
"I'll try a spot of juggling," she said.

Jessica's hair is a little bit messy,
"But my friends look much funnier!"
she thinks.

They're BUSHY and BRISTLY,
SPIKY and FRIZZY,
All coloured red, orange
and pinks.

Hooray! They've found a trampoline,
It's sure to raise a grin.

The giraffe takes flight,
And the hippo's a sight,
As they **LEAP** and

BOUNCE and **SPRING.**

Night night,
JESSICA

Jessica is ready to head back home,
As night eclipses the day.
But there's still time,
For a little more rhyme,
As her friends have
SOMETHING TO
SAY....

She's fun!
She's clever!
She's friendly!
She's kind!
She really loves to play!

Jessica can't deny,
As she waves goodbye,

Jessica, now draw your different friends and tell us why they're so special.